big & SMALL

Original Korean text by Mi-hye Kim
Illustrations by Yun-jeong Shim
Korean edition © Aram Publishing

This English edition published by big & SMALL in 2016
by arrangement with Aram Publishing
English text edited by Joy Cowley
English edition © big & SMALL 2016

Distributed in the United States and Canada by
Lerner Publishing Group, Inc.
241 First Avenue North
Minneapolis, MN 55401 U.S.A.
www.lernerbooks.com
ISBN: 978-1-925249-01-9
Printed in Korea

Day and Night

Written by Mi-hye Kim
Illustrated by Yun-jeong Shim
Edited by Joy Cowley

It was morning.
The sun beamed light
on Ari's house and called,
"Are you still sleeping?"

Ari flung open her windows.
"Good morning, Sun!
I am awake and dressed.
It is good to see you again."

Ari came out to the yard.
"Look, Sun! It's a caterpillar!"

The sun said, "With my light,
you can see small things
closeup and far away."

Ari went to the park.
She played all day and had fun
with her friends.

When it was getting dark,
Ari went back home.

The sun slowly sank
behind the hills in the west.
"Where are you going, Sun?"

"I'm not going anywhere,"
the sun replied. "I'm always
in the same place here in space."

13

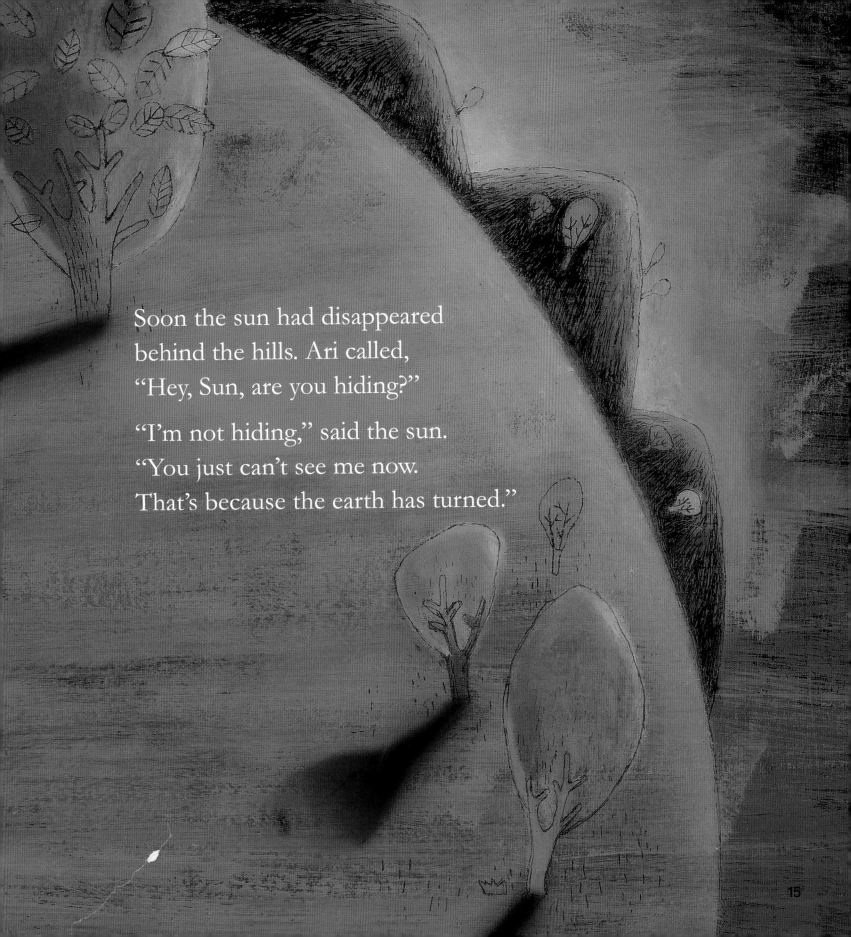

Soon the sun had disappeared
behind the hills. Ari called,
"Hey, Sun, are you hiding?"

"I'm not hiding," said the sun.
"You just can't see me now.
That's because the earth has turned."

15

Then the sun told Ari,
"The earth spins around
once every day.
You'll see me again
tomorrow morning."

The sky became dark.
All sunlight was gone.
It was now night.

Ari could not see the garden.
She could not see anything
because all sunlight was gone.

In the night sky,
stars twinkled and sparkled.
Night creatures made loud sounds
in the dark. *Hoot-hoot! Croak-croak!*

Ari yawned and said,
"Good night, caterpillar.
Good night, Mom and Dad.
Good night, Sun.
I'll see you all in the morning."
Then she went to sleep.

25

When Ari woke up the next morning,
the sun was rising in the east.
The world had turned and
Ari's house was in front of the sun
once again.

Why Do We Have Day and Night?

The earth turns around at the same speed every day. It is the rotation of the earth. We have day and night because of this rotation. Let's find out how this works. You will need a spinning globe of the world and a flashlight.

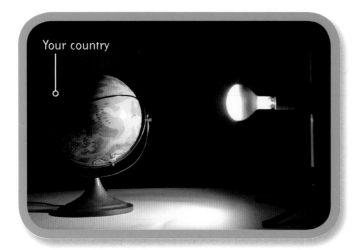

Your country

Night

Hold the flashlight still. Turn the globe until the flashlight is on another part of the globe. Your country is now in darkness. The earth spins slowly and steadily. After several hours, your country will face the sun again.

Morning

Pretend the flashlight is the sun. Find your country on the globe and shine the flashlight on it. See how your country is lit up?

Your country

As the earth turns, some parts will be in the sun, and others will not. It will be day in the areas with sunlight, and it is night without it. That is why day and night occur at different times, from country to country.

Afternoon

As the earth slowly turns, your country moves away from the sun. Soon it will get dark and become night.

Your country

Your country

Midday

Your country on the globe faces the sun. Now it is daytime.

What Is the Earth's Rotation?

Why Does the Sun Rise in the East?

The earth spins from west to east. This makes the sun appear to rise in the east. Then it appears to set in the west. But the sun does not move at all. It looks as though it moves, because our planet rotates.

Why Don't We Feel Dizzy When the Earth Is Spinning?

We spin with the earth. Gravity is a force that keeps us stuck to the ground. The earth constantly spins at the same speed. Because the speed is constant, we do not get dizzy. To feel dizzy, we need to feel a change in motion.

What Would Happen If the Earth Stopped Spinning?

If the earth stopped spinning, one part of the world would have day for six months. The other part would have night for six months. This is because the earth would still orbit around the sun. One part of the planet would be too hot, and the other part would be too cold. This would make it hard for humans and creatures to live on Earth.

Why Are Days Longer in Summer and Shorter in Winter?

The earth is tilted on its axis. This is an imaginary line running from the North Pole to the South Pole. During the earth's orbit around the sun, parts of the planet receive different amounts of sunlight. The half that is tilted toward the sun has summer. The days are longer as the planet's half is in the sunlight longer. The planet's other half is tilted away from the sun. It has its winter season. It receives less sunlight and has shorter days.

Summer

Winter

Day and Night

Each morning the sun appears to rise in the east. Daylight covers the land. Then after many hours, the sun appears to set in the west. The night is very dark. But the sun does not move at all. It is really the earth moving that causes day and night.

Let's think!

How does light help you see things?

Why is it hard to see in the dark?

Why do some animals come out at night?

Why do some animals move around during the day?

Let's do!

Let's take a look at how the earth moves. Watch a shadow change during the day. Its changes show you that the earth is spinning away from the sun.

Put a tall object, such as a cereal box, outside in the sunlight. Record the time of day it is. Measure the object's shadow with a ruler. Check on the object each hour for several hours. Measure the shadow each time. How does it change? What do the changes show you?